Winston the Walrus

Heather L. Kelly

Illustrated by: Sheena Clemons

DEDICATION

Heather L. Kelly: I would like to dedicate this to Oliver and Michael, to my parents Bonnie and David, and to the greatest teachers: Jody Densford, Christina Rodriguez, and Kevin Gose. And of course to my sister and illustrator: Sheena.

Sheena Clemons: For Bailey, Daniel, mom and dad . Thanks to Heather for making this possible.

Winston was a walrus but his friends Peter, Popper, and Peach were penguins.

Every morning Winston's father would wake him up for breakfast and before he could finish, Peach would be at the front door.

"Mr. Winston's dad, can Winston come out to play?"

And every day Winston and Peach would go find Peter and Popper to swim or fish or play hide and seek.

One morning Winston was finishing his breakfast when all of his friends showed up.

"Oh Winston!" exclaimed Peter. "We've found the coolest place!"

"It's a cave!" squealed Popper excitedly.

"But not just any cave," said Peach. "It's got pretty, sparkly ice and pools of water; it's fantastic!"

Winston jumped up, "Let's go!"

Winston followed the penguins for a ways until they came upon a huge ice rock.

"Here it is!" screamed Peter, pointing to the rock.

"Where?" said Winston.

"Here!" said Peach as she wiggled into a tiny opening at the bottom of the rock. Peter and Popper followed her in.

Winston sat there, staring at the opening.

He put a flipper up to it, sighing.

He wasn't going to fit.

He could hear Peter, Popper, and Peach laughing and playing inside the cave.

"Come on Winston! Join us!" the penguins called out.

"I don't feel good. I'm going home."
Winston was ashamed he couldn't fit. He didn't want to tell his friends.

"Oh no! said Peach. "Feel better soon!"

Each day after this, Peach would come to get Winston in the morning and he would tell her he didn't feel well.

"But we're going to the cave. And you still haven't seen it!"

"Well, I don't care about that silly cave," said Winston.

"Fine then," said Peach, hurt. Several days passed and she didn't come back.

All this time Winston's father had been watching carefully. He knew something had happened to make Winston act this way toward his friends.

Winston's father found Winston crying in his room. "Winston, what happened?" Winston told his father about the cave and how he couldn't fit and how it had made him feel bad.

"Winston, you shouldn't be ashamed of who you are. You are a walrus. Walruses don't fit into all the places penguins can, and that's okay. I'm sure your friends never meant to leave you out. If you tell them what's wrong, I think they'll understand."

Winston went to the cave and called out to his friends. He explained why he hadn't been playing with them. "I'm sorry I was mean. I was ashamed."

"Oh Winston," said Peach.
"We love you!" said Popper.
"And we'd rather be with you than go to a cave!" said Peter.

From that day forward, Winston made sure to tell his friends how he was feeling and to always be proud of who he was. Winston was proud to be a walrus. And Peter, Popper, and Peach were proud to be Winston's friends.

Made in the USA
Lexington, KY
13 February 2017